John H. Hopkins

Autobiography in Verse

John H. Hopkins

Autobiography in Verse

ISBN/EAN: 9783337119256

Printed in Europe, USA, Canada, Australia, Japan

Cover: Foto ©Raphael Reischuk / pixelio.de

More available books at **www.hansebooks.com**

Autobiography in Verse:

DEDICATED TO

My Children.

BY THE RT. REV.

JOHN H. HOPKINS, D.D., LL.D.,

BISHOP OF VERMONT.

PRINTED FOR THE FAMILY,

ON THE OCCASION

OF THE

Golden Wedding.

RIVERSIDE PRESS,

CAMBRIDGE.

Introduction.

LD age at length has come, but firm and
    hale,
    Although my seventy years have long
    been passed,
As yet the senses do not seem to fail,
And may, perhaps, for future service last.

Time has impressed no furrows on my brow,
Dark hair still lingers midst the locks of gray,
The upright form has not begun to bow,
Nor do my steps the want of strength betray.

The eye can yet the midnight page explore,
Music its pleasure to the ear can bring,
The hand can paint from Nature, as of yore,
And strike in harmony the tuneful string.

The powers of speech, articulate and clear,
With voice of youthful vigor yet remain;
Nor do the mental faculties appear
To lose their mastery o'er the subject brain.

1

The memory, faithful to a fair degree,
Imagination, prompt and active still,
And judgment, trained so long the truth to see,
Are all obedient to the sovereign will.

But more than these, the heart — affection's
        shrine —
Can yet the warmth of pure emotion prove,
Reflect the glory of the law divine,
And feel the force of sympathy and love.

And when the round of circumstance I view,
How dear the prospect to the grateful soul!
A family so large, so fond and true,
With not one worthless member in the whole!

The precious wife of youth, so kindly spared
To bless my age, in vigor like my own ; —
A numerous band of children, all prepared
To bow in worship at the Saviour's throne ;

With talent and with energy endued,
By Christian education well refined,
Devoted to the useful and the good,
And fairly formed in body and in mind ; —

Grandchildren too, of various ages, rise,
Some haply married, some in nurses' arms ;

And great-grandchildren glad my aged eyes
With the pure beauty of their infant charms!

What monarch can more precious wealth survey?
What mortal lot more favored can be found?
What brighter blessings can the world display?
What better gifts declining years surround?

And when to these I add the special grant
Of highest office in the Church below;
The kind supply of every moderate want;
The smile of welcome wheresoe'er I go;

The fair success of authorship; the voice
Of warm affection and of partial praise:
How should my heart with gratitude rejoice
In all the goodness which has marked my days!

To Christ, the glorious Lord of light and life,
My poor acknowledgments alone are due;
For He has led me through temptation's strife,
The path of truth and duty to pursue.

Some trials, toils, and sorrows I have known,
Some labors which the world might call severe;
False lights to error sometimes lured me on:
But still His guardian Providence was there!

A sinner like the rest, in thought and deed,
No merit of my own can I proclaim ;
His grace alone has caused me to succeed ;
Let all the praise be to His holy Name !

And now, by filial urgency impelled,
I leave this record of my life behind,
To mark the changes which those years beheld,
From youth to age, with fair and candid mind.

Though but an outline, drawn in homely rhyme,
It may the value of Religion prove,
To be, in every circumstance and time,
The only guide to comfort, peace, and love.

Canto First.

 LOVELY city, known to fame,
Of Dublin bears the ancient name ;
Where Manhood's strength and Beauty's
    smile
Claim honor for the Emerald Isle,
The fair Hibernia ! from whose strand
A stalwart race to every land
Has gone, its vigor to impart,
With ready hand and generous heart.

'T was there my earliest breath I drew,
In seventeen hundred ninety-two ;
When January's wintry sway
Had entered on its thirtieth day.

My father was to commerce bred ;
But fortune never raised his head
Above the crowd who toil in vain,
The prize of affluence to obtain.
My mother had a form and face
Endowed with far superior grace,

While talents of no common kind
Shone brightly in her active mind.
Both were quite musical, and made
A fair duet; the flute was played
With the piano. In those days
Pleyel enjoyed the general praise;
Though Haydn and Mozart could claim
A higher and more lasting fame.
But I remember well the power
Of those sweet sounds, as, many an hour,
I proved the charm of Music's sway,
While I upon the carpet lay,
And felt, entranced, their tuneful art
Sink deep into my childish heart!
No other fruit their union graced.
My mother her affections placed
On me, her only offspring. She
Resolved that all her powers should be
Devoted to the precious task
Of my instruction. None could ask
A better teacher. Sooth to say,
Her labor was not thrown away.
'T was said by all that I possessed
Her features, and a mind impressed
With the same gifts and talents rare,
Which made her toil a pleasing care.
To some extent 't was doubtless true:
But it is certain that I drew

From her instruction all the skill
Which forms the thought and guides the will,
So far as knowledge can be given
Without the special light of Heaven.

She led me through the usual round
Of English schools. The classic ground
Of Shakspeare, Dryden, Pope, was spread
Before my eight-years' age was sped.
In music, Haydn's Symphonies
I learned to execute with ease ;
And drawing-lessons did their part
To train the eye and hand for art :
While French was drilled into my tongue,
Because 't was flexible and young.

This was precocious, yet it came
With little effort and no blame.
A solitary child — alone —
Amongst my elders I was thrown.
I had no brother to employ
My hours in boyish sport and joy :
My chief companion through the day
Was my own mother. All the play
With ball, and top, and hoop, and kite,
Could give my spirits no delight
Without associates. Hence I took
My favorite pleasure in my book ;

As soon as I could learn to read,
The habit grew my mind to feed
On stories, pictures, music, till
The thirst for knowledge ruled my will ;
While tales of love, romance, and crime
Made me feel old before my time.
All childish books beyond my reach,
And rarely hearing childish speech,
My boyish intellect became
Too thoughtful for my growing frame.

My mother had no need to press
My studies.   'T was my happiness
To meet the labors of the way,
And make advances day by day.
The toil which other children viewed
With strong dislike, to me seemed good.
And thus I gained, in early life,
Without compulsion, care, or strife,
That mastery o'er each mental power,
Which aids me to the present hour.

My parents both maintained their claim
To the Established Church, in name ;
And I was brought, with formal care,
To have my infant Baptism there.
But piety had little part,
That I could see, in either heart.

Their course was guided by the rule
Laid down in worldly custom's school;
Though late in life they learned to prove
The value of their Saviour's love.
My childhood's thoughts towards heaven to guide,
The grandmother their place supplied.
Fondly she pointed out the way,
And taught my youthful lips to pray.
Thanks be to God! the light thus gained
Through all my earthly course remained,
And held a pure and strong control
O'er the worst perils of the soul.

But now, when my eighth year had passed,
My father deemed it wise to cast
His lot on that far distant shore,
Where, during several years before,
An elder brother, with his wife,
Had chosen to spend their future life.

In August, eighteen hundredth year,
We saw with joy New York appear;
And thence we passed, with brief delay,
Where Philadelphia's city lay.
My uncle there had fixed his home,
In hope of prosperous days to come.
But lavish hand and kindly heart
With prudence had so little part,

That neither wealth nor honors came
To dignify his humble name.

The money which my father brought
Was soon expended.   Then he sought
Some occupation to obtain,
And found his efforts all in vain.
Thus disappointed in his course,
My mother was his last resource.
Well fitted, with accomplished mind,
And manner polished and refined,
She oped at once a ladies' school.
The formal round of stated rule
Was not her forte, but for the rest
Her adaptation was confessed.
Few with such talents could be found ;
She had been trained on maxims sound :
Despising all pretence and show,
Her pupils learned the truth to know.
Their whole deportment she could mould,
And all their faculties unfold,
Till old and young combined to raise
A cordial tribute to her praise.

'T was not the fashion of that day
For female knowledge to display
A competition with the plan
Adopted for the mind of man.

No mathematics were desired,
No Latin and no Greek required;
Nor were the College honors sought,
To crown the girlish powers of thought.

I doubt the wisdom of the change
Which thrusts our females on a range
Of studies so severe and dry.
Their time 't were better to apply
In reading history, travels, poems,
From well-established standard tomes;
And learning every gentle art
Which gilds the home and cheers the heart.

My mother's school was not the place
Where I could run the classic race;
And though reluctant, I was sent,
With all my mind on knowledge bent,
To an academy of boys, —
A scene quite new! At first their noise,
Their boisterous play, and words impure
Were more than I could well endure.
But though by habit reconciled,
And by example oft beguiled,
My conscience still had frequent sway,
And led me, when alone, to pray,
That He who marked each passing hour
Would guard me by His mighty power.

The master of this classic school
Made an exception to his rule
In certain favors which, to me,
Were proofs of partiality.
He had a library well stocked,
And, for the most part, closely locked :
But to my hands the key he gave,
And thus enabled me to save
The hours my youthful schoolmates spent
In idle sports and merriment.
To his piano my access
Was also free.   The game of chess
He taught to me and to his son,
Whose boyish friendship I had won :
And so, without a tear or sigh,
Three years from home passed quickly by.

My studies were an easy task,
Nor could my partial teachers ask
A pupil whose improvement drew
More praise in all he had to do.
Those were the days when Latin claimed
A round of toil now rarely named.
The Grammar mastered in each part —
Its forms and rules well learned by heart —
" Cordery's Colloquies " came next,
And then Cornelius Nepos' text.
" Erasmus' Dialogues " their place

Assumed, with wit and humorous grace:
Selections, from historians drawn,
Next led the youthful student on,
By just gradations, to engage
The harder themes of Cæsar's page,
Sallust and Cicero.   The range
Of study then commenced a change
To classic poets.   Ovid came,
Virgil and Horace ; while the name
Of Tacitus, in portions meet,
And Livy, made our course complete.

But the main feature of the plan,
Which still through all this reading ran,
Was *writing exercises.*   There,
The pupil's work was most severe,
And most effective.   In the mass
Of recitation by the class,
The small display which each could make
Might 'scape detection of mistake.
While *writing* Latin plainly showed
His true position on the road
Of classic learning, and displayed
The actual progress he had made.

The thorough strictness of that day,
If not entirely passed away,
Is rarely found in modern schools.

And yet 't is clear, that, by those rules,
The mind was trained to use its powers
With great effect.   The studious hours,
Bestowed upon a language dead,
Demand a cool reflecting head,
The laws of grammar to descry,
Its rules minutely to apply,
And give a *reason* for each word
Employed the meaning to record.
The *judgment* thus acquires, at length,
A high degree of force and strength ;
The *habit* of research and thought
Is to its best condition brought ;
The power of *application* gains
A mastery which through life remains ;
And, through this discipline of youth,
Prepares the *man* to seek for truth.
He learns *to think*, and that once known,
The most important task is done.

The great result which boys attain
By classic lore, is not the gain
Of the mere language, which no more
Is used by scholars, as before,
In speech and letters ; though its force
Is felt throughout the student's course,
In all the intellectual range
Of learning, spite of time or change.

Nor is it in the facts acquired
From Roman authors, so admired :
Since they are all translated well,
And may their tales in English tell.
But 't is the discipline of mind
In which its greatest use we find ;
And in this aspect of the case,
It claims a high peculiar place.

Yet this most just and worthy praise
Is seldom due in modern days,
Since the old discipline has lost
Its vigor, to the pupil's cost ;
For now a labor-saving mode
Of hasty progress takes the road,
Content with superficial show
Substantial learning to forego,
And thus contriving, by its plan,
To *please* the boy, and *spoil* the man.

Canto Second.

T Bordentown, a village fair,
Upon the River Delaware,
My years of Latin studies passed:
But as my kind preceptor cast
His library before my sight,
It was my pleasure and delight
To spend my free and vacant hours,
With all my fresh and youthful powers,
In reading through the varied round
Of English books which there I found.
The British Drama, all complete,
The Poets, lords of Fancy's seat,
The best Historians, works on Art
And Medicine, formed the greater part.
For novels there was little room;
Their palmy days had yet to come.
But Fielding, Smollett, and the fair
Burney and Radcliffe, all were there;
Cervantes and the " Arabian Nights,"
In which the boyish taste delights,
With many others.   Through the mass

I made my leisure time to pass,
And thus contrived a larger gain
Of general reading to attain,
Than I have ever known belong
To any at an age so young.

And yet I do not mean to say
That I was never found at play.
When school was out, I daily went
To take a share in merriment,
And learned the average show of skill
In boyish games, with right good will.
But little time in this employ
Was spent. It gave no solid joy.
My thoughts on other subjects ran,
More fitted to the mind of man.
I loved to be alone with books,
And often wandered by the brooks
Which wound their mazy, babbling way
To where the noble river lay;
Yet still alone with Nature's face,
Marking its beauty and its grace: —
The waves which on their courses run,
Sparkling like diamonds in the sun;
The clouds which, morn and eve, unfold
The hues of crimson and of gold;
The wild-flowers in their drapery meet,
Which sprang so freshly round my feet;

2

The varied foliage of the trees ;
The birds that carolled at their ease ; —
Unwitting that the day would come
When railways there should make their home,
And all the charming scene, which quite
Entranced, at times, my gazing sight,
Should be invaded by the band
Which Commerce sends throughout the land, —
Friend to its business and its wealth,
But foe, full oft, to peace and health, —
Friend to its progress, power, and art,
But foe to thoughts which fill the heart,
Inspiring, by their high control,
The loftier visions of the soul !

But now another change drew nigh.
My mother, with a careful eye
To the completion of her plan,
In all that fits the gentleman,
Sent me to Princeton, to reside
With a French refugee, whose pride
Of *old nobility*, 't was said,
Was forced to stoop and earn his bread
By giving lessons to a few
In dancing and in fencing too.
These arts for me she much desired,
By polished Europe so admired.
Besides, the pure Parisian speech

He was well qualified to teach ;
And thus my knowledge of that tongue
Would be secured while I was young.

In this French family I spent
Almost a year, with mind intent
On making progress, day by day,
In all that now before me lay.
I danced and fenced with easy skill,
But books were all my favorites still.
Of these my teacher seldom thought ;
No library could there be sought,
Yet some stray volumes were by chance
Preserved, when he arrived from France.
Rousseau, Marmontel, and Molière,
With Voltaire's works, in part, were there.
Of these I mastered all I could,
And found them yield more harm than good,
Save in the thorough knowledge gained
Of French, which has through life remained,
And done some service, when my mind
Became to better works inclined.

My mother's school had prospered been
In Trenton.   But a different scene
Was now to open, when she moved
To Philadelphia.   There I proved
Of some assistance in the art

Which drawing-lessons best impart,
By making patterns for her class.
But still I ceased not to amass
My fund of learning. Every day
Some teacher led my onward way.
In mathematics and in Greek
My knowledge I had yet to seek ;
And these I studied, though with less
Of zeal, but yet with fair success.
In music, too, advance was made.
The violin with ease I played,
Enough at least my part to bear
In concerts, where a certain share
Of harmony is needed still,
Without a marked display of skill.

About this time, a partial friend,
Who loved his evening hours to spend
In music, thought that there should be
An Amateur Society,
In whose performance might appear
Sufficient art to please the ear,
With good Quartets, and, by degrees,
With some of Haydn's Symphonies.

The plan succeeded, and we came,
Our Constitution's rules to frame.
Flutes, violins, and clarionets,

Tenors, bassoons, and flageolets
Were represented, and a brace
Of good French horns were in their place ;
But no bass viol!   What to do,
In this dilemma, no one knew,
Until I undertook to try
If I could not the want supply.

I hired an instrument, and took
A master and instruction-book,
Without delay.   And when the hour
Arrived for our first notes of power,
The month allotted to prepare
Was found sufficient.   All were there,
And my *début* was not the least
In the enjoyment of our feast.
Success inspired me with good will
To practise with industrious skill ;
And in those concerts many a night
Was passed with genuine delight :
Nor have I yet forgot the art
With which I played that youthful part.

But our Society had few,
Save Frenchmen, whom by name I knew.
My French and music both combined
To make them feel at once inclined
Towards more companionship with me

Than suited with morality.
Loose and licentious in their talk,
I was compelled their zeal to balk ;
And only saw their faces when
The concert-night come round again.

Haply for me, my mother's school
Had brought me under better rule.
Her pupils' families embraced
A circle by refinement graced ;
The sisters and the brothers there
Gave me a kind and cordial share
Of friendly welcome. I was led
To go to church, for they were bred
Episcopalians. Bishop White,
At old St. Peter's, met my sight ;
And his assistant, with whose son
An intimacy soon begun.
Thus I was placed within a round
Of social converse, where I found
The highest kind of moral tone
Which cities might expect to own.
As yet religion could impart
No deep emotion to my heart;
But taste and habit both forbade
Of youthful vice the slightest shade ;
And from its gross and noxious sway
In strong disgust I turned away.

Amongst those families were two,
Whose heads were merchants.   To pursue
The walks of commerce ne'er had been
My choice.   But now that I had seen
Its fair results amongst those friends,
I felt the force which kindness lends ;
And when they offered me a place,
I took the post with cheerful face,
Although my mother gave consent
With great reluctance.   Thus I went
Into the counting-house, and there
Passed one whole year, with little care
Of toil or business.   It was said
That foreign commerce all lay dead
Through Jefferson's Embargo, planned
With no advantage to the land.
And as my kind employers made
Their profits by the shipping trade,
I had no object to pursue,
Because there was no work to do.
My post of duty I could hold,
And did whatever I was told.
But that was little.   Long before
The year was out, the dream was o'er.
My place I purposed to resign ;
A merchants' life could not be mine.

My time now ended, I was free,

And joined a young Society
Called *Philological,* designed
To cultivate the powers of mind,
By compositions and debates,
On every subject which relates
To social life or moral truth,
Tending to elevate the youth
In force of thought and skill of speech,
And well arranged to give to each
A field in which he might display
Such talent as within him lay.

It was my mother's strong desire
That I should to the law aspire.
She was ambitious for her son,
And deemed more honor could be won
By that profession. 'T was the line
In which she thought me born to shine,
And thus attain a lofty name,
Sure of success in wealth and fame.

To this bright scheme, at first, I paid
No great attention. But it made
A deep impression, when I found
How well I could maintain my ground,
Whene'er the task devolved on me
In our new-made Society.
I knew that I could write with ease,

And now discovered, by degrees,
That I had fluency of tongue,
And argued well for one so young.
My frank associates thought they saw
That I was destined for the law,
And in due time my mind became
Persuaded to believe the same.

One night, 't was in my sixteenth year,
A little scene made this appear
More obvious.   By our general plan,
The order of debating ran
In fixed routine.   Before the close
Of every meeting held, we chose
The question for the next debate ;
Two members also, bound to state
The arguments on either side,
Were named, who to the case applied
Such study as they might think meet,
Their preparation to complete.

On this occasion 't was my lot
To open the debate.   I brought
My speech to a successful close,
And my antagonist arose,
But only to apologize ;
An inflammation of his eyes
Had kept him back, though much desired,
From reading what the case required.

It was a fair excuse, of course.
Our chairman, as the next resource,
Called on the members to reply ;
But all were silent, grave, and shy.
An awkward pause ensued, and then
He asked me to begin again,
In hope that this the ice might break,
And others be induced to speak.

I rose and took the vacant place
Of my antagonist.   The case
Was all reversed.   With fluent tongue,
I showed my former speech was wrong ;
And proved, that, in sound reason's sight,
The contrary result was right.

This strange attempt great favor found,
And loud applause was echoed round.
That I " must be a lawyer " went
From mouth to mouth, with one consent ;
Since nothing but a lawyer's mind
Could be so readily inclined
To bend its powers, with easy skill,
On either side, for good or ill.
The little incident became
A passport to some youthful fame,
And it seemed settled, from that day,
That I in law must make my way.

Yet now in this I cannot see
Why such conclusion just should be.
For every mooted question shows
Two sides at least, and he who knows
Enough to weigh them both with care
Can always give a candid share
To either side, if so inclined.
It is an exercise of mind
Required of all who seek the truth,
In hoary age or vigorous youth ;
Although, unhappily, but few
Perform it with the labor due.

Canto Third.

DOMESTIC trials cast a shade,
For years, upon the efforts made
By both my parents. They were free,
So far as I could ever see,
From serious failings, yet their life
Was troubled sadly by the strife
Of discord. Though their course was true
To moral principle, they drew
No comfort from Religion's power,
And took no care to guard each hour
Of social converse by the rule
Which governs in the Christian school, —
The rule of meekness, peace, and love.
Instead of this, they seemed to prove
That trifles light as air may bring,
To tongues unbridled, force to sting.
At length, with alienated heart,
They deemed it best to live apart.
He, as a book-keeper, remained
In Philadelphia. She retained

Her old profession; but 't was planned
That she should move to Maryland;
There she resided for some years,
Familiar with the griefs and tears
Which wait upon the wretched fate
Of those who try the wedded state,
Without a serious thought or care
For wisdom's grace to guide them there.

This separation gave to me
An unrestricted liberty.
And though my heart felt sad and sore,
That I could share their home no more,
Yet was it a relief to know
That discord could no further go.
With me they had no fault to find,
Their words and looks were always kind,
And nothing had occurred to force
Their censure of my filial course.
I saw full well that both were wrong
In thought, in temper, and in tongue.
But 't was not right for me to chide
My parents.   Duty still denied
That I had power to interfere,
Though often, with a silent tear,
I left my seat and sought my room,
To 'scape the bitter strife to come.

Yet now I hoped that Time might bring
Some healing balm upon his wing,
Since I could see no serious cause
To break the band of wedlock's laws.
'T was only temper, mixed with pride,
That brought reproach from either side ;
And I looked forward to the hour
When love might yet resume its power,
And they the rest of life should spend
In peace and concord to the end.
Alas ! that hope proved all in vain,
They never met on earth again !

Some months before the crisis came,
Wilson commenced his work of fame
On Ornithology, and I
Was urged my pencil to apply,
That the engravings might appear
With Nature's colors, true and clear.
That work was lucrative.   My hand
Was rapid, and could well command
Enough for all my wants and more ;
But I cared little for the store
Which from such occupation grew.
A different course, both strange and new,
Was strongly pressed upon my mind,
To which my thoughts at length inclined,

Though I should have preferred by far
To try my fortune at the bar.

Some of the cordial friends I met
Were Scotchmen, all whose views were set,
Without much learning or pretence,
On worldly tact and common sense.
They praised the majesty of law,
But in the lawyer's business saw
So little truth, or honest zeal
For justice, that they could not feel
Content to have my plan of life
Doomed to the work of venal strife,
Where I must sell my hireling tongue,
Without regard to right or wrong ;
My powers with equal care applied,
If only paid, to either side ;
Willing my utmost pains to spend
The vilest culprit to defend ;
And ready still success to prize,
Though gained by sophistry and lies.

This argument had little force
To turn me from my cherished course.
There was no cause, that I could see,
Why lawyers could not honest be.
They were not forced to take a case
Where fraud or villainy had place ;

They might be tempted by a fee,
To that I should of course agree,
But such temptation could be found,
With equal ease, within the round
Of every lot.   The difference lay
In open, public, plain display
Of all the learning, art, and skill,
By which the lawyer works the ill :
' While every other knave can wear
The cloak of secrecy, and dare
The world his baseness to remark,
Because 't is managed in the dark.
But if the lawyer has a heart
Where moral conscience acts its part,
He may withstand the power of gold,
Refusing to be bought or sold,
While he is ever prompt to press
The cause of truth and righteousness.

My Scottish friends, on this, forbore
To urge their censure any more,
But called me to another ground
Of prudence, which was strong and sound.
There was no prospect, as they said,
That I could earn my daily bread,
Until my legal course was spent
For many years.   The general bent
Of young ambition pointed still

To that profession.   Men of skill,
In time, to eminence might rise,
With wealth and fame to greet their eyes.
But these in number were the few,
The rest had little work to do.
The Bar was largely overstocked,
The hopes of hundreds all were mocked
By disappointment.   How could I
Expect my income to supply,
Without some other source of gain,
Those years of struggle to sustain?

Instead of this uncertain strife,
They counselled me to try the life
Of manufacturer.   The field
In this lay open, and would yield
A rich return, and still secure
A maintenance, both safe and sure.
The business they commended most
Was making iron.   England's boast
Was largely based upon her art
In each immense and varied part
Of this vast manufacture.   Here
I might be prospered in a sphere
Where work was needed.   We were still
Dependent upon British skill.
So long as this our wants supplied,
Old England could not be defied;

3

And if we would be truly free,
Her arts must here transplanted be.
On this if I should take my stand,
Honor and wealth I might command.
No praise that legal lore may share
With such distinction could compare,
Since I should couple with my name
A public benefactor's fame !

The views these Scottish friends expressed
Sunk deep into my youthful breast,
Though strongly warring with the force
Which governed all my previous course.
'T was plain the hope I must resign,
That legal honors should be mine.
The furnace and the forge could show
No charms that I desired to know.
The labors of mechanic art
Could neither win my mind nor heart.
My tastes and habits must be changed,
My old associates be estranged,
And all my life be cast anew :
But yet, what better could I do ?
My present occupation led
To nothing more than daily bread.
The plan proposed might ope the way
To fortune at a future day ;
And science and inventive skill,

If guided by a steadfast will,
Might in due time attain the ends
Predicted by my Scottish friends.
With these in prospect, could I think
That fear of toil should make me shrink ?
Should I refuse, on grounds so weak,
The safer path of life to seek,
Because my tastes and habits stood
As barriers to a solid good ?

Such reasoning, by degrees, my mind
To this new enterprise inclined.
My friends prepared a fitting place
In which to start my novel race.
Evans, whose famed inventive skill
Reformed the modern flouring-mill,
Had turned his genius now to try
The steam-engine to simplify ;
And I was taken to his home,
An iron-master to become,
On the broad comprehensive scale
Where art and science might prevail.
Thus launched upon my strange career,
I spent my first laborious year.
It was an easy task to draw
All the machinery I saw ;
I studied hard, with zealous will,
In " Emerson's Mechanics " still :

In Mineralogy I made
A rapid progress, while I paid
To Chemistry a good degree
Of fair and honest industry;
And as it was my cherished plan
To be a scientific man,
While yet the all-important part
Of practice, which belongs to art,
Should be attained with equal care,
I was resolved my time to share
In all the work which, day by day,
Before my observation lay.

Rising each morn before the dawn,
My chosen course of toil went on.
At first I found it hard enough, —
My hands were soft, the work was rough;
But yet I persevered until
I had acquired sufficient skill,
To show the workmen that I knew
All that they were employed to do.

The year was closed with ample praise
From all around me; but to raise
My edifice of art more high,
I deemed it needful to apply
My time and thoughts, as much or more,
To smelting iron from the ore.

A friendly invitation came
In a rich iron-master's name;
So to New Jersey I went on,
Where this important work was done :
And, as before, I spent my hours,
With all my young ambition's powers,
Between my labors and my books ;
While no unkindly words or looks,
From my associates, seemed to say,
That they were weary of my stay.

The following year my steps were bent
To Philadelphia, where I spent
The closing period of my course
With unabated zeal and force,
At a good Foundry.   There and then
I came in contact with some men
Of rank and influence, who came
From South America, to frame
A plan for iron-works, to be
Fixed by their government's decree
On a firm basis, sure to stand,
A credit to their native land.

This scheme was placed before my eyes,
As leader of the enterprise ;
And from that source the notion sprung
That I must learn the Spanish tongue.

So I began, without delay,
To give two hours of every day,
Under a master, with desire,
That noble language to acquire.

My progress went by quick degrees.
In six months' time I read with ease;
But the Commissioners were gone
To other States, my hope had flown !
Doubtless they found a fitter man
To execute their useful plan,
And I was saved for higher aim
Than aught which they had power to name.

My three years' course was done at last;
The age of twenty-one had passed,
When I received an offer new,
More safe and more attractive too.
In eighteen hundred and thirteen,
The land at war one year had been,
And iron-making claimed a store
Of profit never known before.
Our strife with England closed, of course,
All importation from that source,
And iron rose to prices high,
Demanding an increased supply,
When we dependent had become
Upon our factories at home.

A German merchant, forced to quit
His foreign commerce, deemed it fit
To build a furnace, which might yield
Of honest gain a fairer field.
He took a partner to divide
The capital to be supplied.
The place was near to Pittsburgh, where
They hoped a mine of wealth to share.
To guide the work they offered me
A thousand dollars' salary,
Besides a small percentage claim
Upon the profits, — when they came.
The terms were liberal and kind ;
And I at once made up my mind,
With gratitude to God, whose hand
Had given such task to my command.

No time was lost.   I took my way
To where my new-found duty lay.
We built our furnace, and begun
The usual course of work to run :
But the expenses proved too large,
And soon became a weighty charge ;
The firm dissolved, and I was free
To shape afresh my destiny !

Canto Fourth.

NOTHER prospect now arose,
A brighter fortune to disclose.
Among my Pittsburgh friends was one,
Who held a place almost alone, —
The wealthy James O'Hara. He
Proposed a partnership to me
In an old furnace, much decayed,
Which might, he thought, with care be made
A source of profit. He possessed
The land and capital. The rest
Would on my management depend,
To compass a successful end.

On this new sphere I entered now,
With hopeful heart and cheerful brow.
The furnace lands stood, bright and clear,
In the sweet vale of Ligonier.
But soon I found that all my care
Could tend to little profit there.
The market for our iron lay
In Pittsburgh, fifty miles away;

And wagons, on a wretched road,
Were used to bear the heavy load.
The River Conemaugh could bring,
'T was true, for some few days in spring,
A large proportion, when it ran
In a brief freshet. But that plan
Involved delays and dangers too,
With fifteen miles to travel through.
Thus, either way, a serious cost
Of transportation must be lost.
Besides, the ore was poor and dear;
The woods for charcoal were not near;
The buildings all required repair,
And great expense was needed there;
Yet on I toiled, with might and main,
Until the war was over. Then
The price of iron quickly fell,
And I was satisfied full well
That labor, time, and money — all —
Were spent and gone beyond recall!

But in those years a mighty change
Gave to my life a higher range
Of thought and feeling, through the power
Of Him who rules each passing hour,
And shapes the end, in grace and love,
With light and wisdom from above.

One night, while reading, all alone,
A work of Hannah More, there shone
A sudden beam of truth divine,
Which I pretend not to define,
Into my inmost heart.   Its force
Was pure and gentle ; but my course
Seemed from that hour to own its guide
In Christ the Lord, once crucified,
And now MY SAVIOUR, whose control
Had full possession of my soul !

My childhood's rule of private prayer
Had still remained.   Through every snare
Of youth's temptations, it had shed
A guardian influence o'er my head ;
Yet now my thoughts could upwards soar,
With feelings never known before.
Repentance, earnest, deep and new,
Humility, sincere and true,
Faith, in its power of grateful love,
For the first time my heart could prove ;
And from that moment I must date
The change to a converted state.

The practical result ensued,
In trying to produce some good
Among my workmen.   I began
A Sunday service, on the plan

Of social worship in my room,
To which they all were free to come.
I prayed with them, and read the Word,
Exhorting them to seek the Lord.
We were not near to any place
Where they could have the means of grace,
And so I spent the Sabbath hour,
And did the little in my power.

And oft, when times of sickness came,
I raised to health their prostrate frame
With timely medicine, *gratis* given.
For I, some years before, had striven
To learn the noble healing art,
So far at least as might impart
A knowledge of the general rule
Adopted in its highest school.
The books of Reese and Thomas led
My practice.   I recoiled with dread
From quackery.   But it was a road
Of twenty miles to the abode
Where dwelt the doctor.   Hence the will
To exercise my humble skill
Appeared a duty, clear and plain ;
Nor was it exercised in vain !
The Great Physician deigned to bless
My labor with entire success.

My mother's school had now become
Less prosperous. So I brought her home;
And for the next two years she tried
To live in comfort by my side.
But no society was there
In which she could with pleasure share.
Thinking she should be more content
In Philadelphia, there she went,
At her desire, the following year,
When my disastrous days drew near.

But the best earthly boon from heaven,
By Providence, meanwhile, was given, —
A faithful wife ! whose love and truth
Were the bright solace of my youth,
And now, through fifty years and more,
Have cheered my age to near fourscore.

A maiden fair, in Hamburg born,
Whose education might adorn
The loftiest social rank, had come,
Thirteen years old, to find her home
In Baltimore. Her father claimed
Descent from Lutherans much famed,
A learned and ministerial line,
Noted for zeal in things divine.
Himself a merchant, he begun
A prosperous career to run,

With full success, until the day
When war with England drove away
Our foreign commerce, and perforce
Compelled him to a different course.
So, in my neighborhood, he sought
A sheep-farm, where in time he brought
IIis family; and soon I came,
With no intent to light the flame
Of love, for I had yet to earn
My fortune in my new concern,
And thoughts of marriage held no part
In the direction of my heart.

But I remember well the hour
Which led me first to test the power
Of his fair daughter. With a face
And form expressive in the grace
Of maiden beauty, with a hand
Which o'er her harp had full command,
With voice of sweet and thrilling tone,
The soul of music was her own!
Her manners, genial, yet refined,
Showed a pure taste and polished mind;
And when the visit's hour was o'er,
I felt that I had ne'er before
Beheld a face and form so fair,
Uniting gifts so rich and rare!

The admiration thus begun
Proved to be mutual. I won
Her parents' kind regard, while she
Despised the arts of coquetry;
And when I sought her hand, she bent
Her eyes, and, blushing, gave consent.
My course of love was smooth and clear,
Exempt from jealousy or fear;
And in due time a Lutheran priest
Presided at our marriage-feast;
For man and wife we had become,
And then I brought my treasure home.
A precious treasure! Through a life
Which had its share of toil and strife,
She has been constant to employ
Her power for order, peace, and joy;
Intent her duty to pursue,
With heart unselfish, warm, and true!

The time when this event was seen
Was eighteen hundred and sixteen,
The eighth of May. Our life to cheer,
Four days within the following year,
Our first-born child was kindly given
By the indulgent hand of Heaven, —
A lovely daughter! in whose face
The promise of superior grace
Already shone, our hopes to guide,

Until in time 't was verified
By talents and devotion rare,
Which few are privileged to share.

The year before, I had to spend
Some days in court, bound to attend
As witness in a suit at law.
The scene had powerful force to draw
My boyish inclinations back ;
And I resolved my course to track
Towards that profession. I had known
A lawyer in the county-town.
With him to tarry, on my way,
My name to enter from that day
As his law-student, home to ride,
With " Blackstone's Commentaries " tied
Across my saddle, — such the plan
On which I formally began
My legal studies. Though, in fact,
'T was doubtful whether I should act
As practising attorney, still
I had a firm, determined will
To gain the knowledge and the power.
And so I gave each leisure hour
To reading " Blackstone," whom I found
As entertaining as profound.
When from my business tasks released,
His volumes were my daily feast ;

And there were none to which my mind
With livelier interest inclined,
Save only when I would pursue
The learning to religion due.

Two years of study were required
Of all who to the Law aspired;
And eighteen months thus passed away,
When I no longer could delay
To close the furnace.　Since the peace
With England forced all hope to cease,
And foreign iron could be bought
For half our price, I soon was taught,
By sheer necessity, to shape
Some other course, and so escape
The ruin of my last design,
While youth and energy were mine.

I sought my honored partner's face,
To lay before him all the case.
It was a heavy bill of cost, —
Full twenty thousand dollars lost!
The half belonged to me, 't was true,
But I had nothing, as he knew.
The sad result was clearly shown, —
He had to bear the load alone,
Until, at some far distant day,
I might, perhaps, my share repay.

For this result, however hard,
He was in some degree prepared.
For I had never used disguise,
Nor failed to strengthen all the ties
Of honest confidence and truth,
Confessing the mistakes of youth
Whene'er they happened to arise,
And keeping still before his eyes,
Subject to his more wise control,
A faithful statement of the whole.

Yet though I fully understood
That I had done the best I could,
And, with integrity of heart,
Had ever tried to fill my part,
Still I was conscious that the end
Might turn away this valued friend.
A loss so large few men could bear.
The luckless agent few would spare.
Reproach, suspicion, censure, blame,
My faults and errors would proclaim;
And I might have to tell the tale
So common to the men who fail !

But I no trace of this could find
In James O'Hara's generous mind.
My hand with cordial grasp he held,
And all my fears at once dispelled.

4

No look of coldness met my eye,
No censure marked his kind reply;
No lack of confidence was there.
The loss he would contrive to bear,
And I alone should have my way,
To close the works without delay,
And in my course should still depend
On him as on a steadfast friend.

Relieved, and ready to depart,
I wrung his hand with swelling heart,
My thanks scarce able to repeat
That I such kind regard should meet.
But through my life I never knew
A soul more noble, just, and true;
And ne'er, while memory holds her place,
Can time his generous acts efface.

With fervent gratitude to God,
I soon commenced my homeward road;
But ere I left, it was my care
For my next dwelling to prepare.

There was a prosperous female school,
Conducted by the careful rule
Of an instructress, patronized
By all who solid merit prized.
With her a contract fair I made;

My youthful wife was to be paid
For teaching music, while my part
Was to give lessons in the art
Of drawing. A commodious room
Was our apartment to become,
And then our daily board should be
In common with the family.

My iron-business now to close
Required some weeks.   With small repose
I toiled to balance each account,
Till all were paid the full amount.
My personal property was sold
At auction, and the product told
Upon the settlement of debt ;
But no dissatisfaction met
My ears, except in words of woe
That we were thus obliged to go.
Our work, throughout the country round,
Had been of great advantage found ;
Though loss to us, to them 't was gain,
And hence the parting gave some pain
To many, while there were a few
Who marked with tears their sad adieu !

At length the day prefixed drew near,
When we should leave sweet Ligonier :
And there was sorrow in that hour !

'T was here that we had felt the power
Of wedded love, and parents' joy;
'T was here I labored to employ
My best affections for the Lord,
Worthy alone to be adored;
'T was here I used my humble art
To cheer with hope the poor man's heart;
'T was here my precious wife and I
Admired, with fond artistic eye,
The beauties of pure Nature's face
In all their native forms of grace,
Wandering together o'er the scene
By murmuring brook and valley green;
And here were some who warmly kept
Our memory, and sincerely wept,
With bitter grief, upon the day
That sent us on our devious way!

Canto Fifth.

RRIVED in Pittsburgh (then a town
Of small extent, though much renown,
The population it could boast
Some eighteen thousand at the most),
Our child, her precious nurse, and I
At once proceeded to comply
With the kind offer which had come,
To make our temporary home
At my late partner's dwelling.   There,
We found the most endearing care
And cordial welcome from his wife,
A lady now in middle life,
With queenly face and active mind,
And manner frank, though quite refined,
Who was, as all around me said,
Of good society the head.
Her daughters, gracious, kind, and bright,
Petted our babe with much delight,
In which their mother's genial heart
Was pleased to bear an ample part

While our loved host, with cheerful word,
Presided at the social board,
Dispensing anecdotes and wit,
As if he felt it right and fit
That youthful hope should have its sway,
And all our griefs be driven away !

His generous stand, so nobly shown,
On every side was fully known ;
And sympathy and kindness grew
Apace amongst the friends we knew.
How sweet such goodness to recall !
The hand of God was o'er it all !

The new arrangement soon was made,
My drawing-class with zeal arrayed
Their ready pencils, and the sound
Of that dear harp was floated round,
With voice melodious, giving more
Delight than aught they felt before,
And charming every youthful heart
With music's pure enchanting art. ·
Our residence was at the school ;
But 't was a fixed and constant rule
That every Saturday should see
Our lovely babe, my wife, and me
At my late partner's, there to dine
And taste his goodly ale and wine.

Nor was this all.   He deemed it meet
To give me a commodious seat
In his own office, there to stay,
And keep his books from day to day;
While I must to his table come,
And know that I had there a home.

This was a friendly scheme, devised
In kindness, which I highly prized.
The books thus placed within my power
Scarce claimed the care of half an hour;
And I, in quiet and alone,
Could call the office-room my own,
And study law with all the zeal
Which fervent industry could feel.

There were two leaders at the Bar
Of Pittsburgh, whose repute by far
Exceeded all the rest.   Of these
One lawyer, whom I chanced to please,
Gave me, with kind and liberal grace,
The offer of a student's place,
Loaned me his books, and when desired,
Taught me whatever I required.
Six months were wanting to complete
My two years' study, and to meet
The grave examination, made
Before my name could be displayed

As an Attorney. Every hour
Was well devoted, with the power
Of stern necessity, which wrought
The strongest stimulus of thought.

The day at length arrived, when I
My new profession could apply
In legal practice. Nothing loath,
I took the lawyer's formal oath
With Christian seriousness, and faith
That I should keep it unto death.
The Court, as was the custom, gave
The case of a poor thievish knave
Who had no counsel, to my care ;
But no defensive ground was there :
The proof was positive and plain.
What credit could I hope to gain
In such a hopeless cause as this ?
And yet it was not wise to miss
The opportunity assigned
By order of the Court. My mind
Was all confused when I began
To argue for the guilty man ;
And when I closed, I could not tell
If I had spoken ill or well.
But though the culprit, at the time,
Received the just reward of crime,
My speech, it seemed, was praised by all

The crowd that occupied the hall.
Some lawyers, too, in kindness came,
To prophesy my future fame ;
And I went home to cheer my wife,
With this first tale of legal life.

That precious wife, admired, beloved
By those that knew her, always proved
My faithful helpmate.   Prompt to bear,
In every cross, her ample share ;
Warmly devoted to her friends ;
Above all low and selfish ends ;
With active energy of will,
Guided by pure affection still ;
Her head might sometimes be at fault,
Her heart was never !   When I thought
How rarely wedded life is blest
With comfort such as mine possessed, —
How vain must wealth and fame become
When discord blights the peace of home, —
How cheerless each domestic art
Where true religion has no part, —
I could not find fit words of praise
To Him who thus had crowned my days
With such a priceless treasure given
By the all-gracious hand of Heaven !

Our school engagements now were done,

And I my lawyer's life begun
In a small dwelling, just behind
The Court-House. I gave up my mind
To study and to business there,
With unremitting zeal and care,
And earned enough, from day to day,
For all our moderate wants to pay,
Since the employment of that year
Produced a thousand dollars clear.
But I had overtasked my power
By hard night reading. To the hour
Of two, each morning, o'er the page
It was my custom to engage
My weary eyes and throbbing brain,
Until at length a fearful train
Of symptoms made me understand
That fell Consumption was at hand.

I had a skilful doctor nigh,
Who watched me with a friendly eye,
And often warned me of the end
Which must this ill-judged course attend.
My anxious wife, the point to gain,
Had still remonstrated in vain.
But now her father came to town,
To take the child and mother down
On a short visit. Then, to aid
The new resolve that I had made,

A favorite trotting horse he sent,
On which one hour each morn I spent
Before my breakfast; while, instead
Of two o'clock, I laid my head
Upon my pillow at eleven,
The rule by my physician given.
This plan was followed day by day,
And all the danger passed away,
Through His kind favor who had still
Preserved me from each dreaded ill, —
That gracious Lord who holds control
Over the body and the soul!

The leading church in Pittsburgh, then,
Was Presbyterian, and the strain
Of preaching, long established there,
Was Calvinistic, strict and fair.
My former partner's family
On Sundays took my wife and me
To their own pew, and we inclined
With them to harmonize our mind.
She, both in worship and in word,
Could well with those dear friends accord ;
While I had nothing to object
Against that much respected sect.

Another far less numerous band
Held the Episcopalian stand.

And these had then a genial man
As Rector, who his course began
With great acceptance : warm of heart,
Cordial of speech, skilled to impart
The tone of cheerfulness to all
With whom he chanced each day to fall,
And lately wedded to a wife
Of winning grace and blameless life.

A mutual friendship, strong, though new,
'Twixt them and us full quickly grew,
Which aided greatly to define
The Christian course of me and mine.

One day he told me he had bought
An organ for his Church, but sought
Without success, though long he tried,
To have the organist supplied,
And then suggested that I might
Relieve him from his painful plight,
If I would occupy the ground,
Until some other could be found.
He hoped I might the task approve,
Though it must be a work of love ;
For no reward should I conclude,
Except the sense of doing good.

This set me thinking of the hours

In which I cherished Music's powers,
From childhood up to manhood's prime,
Devoting no small zeal and time
To play three instruments with skill,
Composing waltzes, songs, at will,
And ranging through a circle wide
Of harmony, on every side,
While not one effort had been given
To make it serve the cause of Heaven!
Yet music formed a grand display
In worship at King David's day.
The Psalms were written to be sung
By choirs devout, with faithful tongue ;
And psalteries, trumps, and cornets' sound
Gave aid to spread the chorus round.
The great St. Paul full plainly told
The Church on earth her strains to hold;
And golden harps and hymns of love
Reëcho through the Church above.
How could I, then, with grace deny
My help this music to supply?
If God had granted me the art,
Should He not claim its better part?
And was it not high time to share
The talent with His house of prayer?

Concluding thus the post to take,
And hence decided to forsake

The Presbyterians, though my mind
Had then no fault with them to find,
I told my wife that she was free
To stay with them, or go with me.
She did not like the change, and tried
One Sunday, parted from my side.
But that was all! The next she came,
And, standing near the organ frame,
United in our sacred song
With thrilling voice and grateful tongue.
In three brief months, we knelt to prove
The promise of our Saviour's love
Before the Sacramental Board;
Together taking, at His word,
The holy consecrated sign
Of sacrifice, through grace divine,
For a lost world in mercy given,
To save us, by His blood, for Heaven!
And thus the Church became our home,
From thence, through life, no more to roam;
Although as yet I could not trace
Her special Apostolic place,
And needed study, thought, and care,
A just conclusion to prepare.

Canto Sixth.

BEFORE my year of practice closed had
been,
A second daughter entered on the scene.
The next year saw us in a house more fair,
As business came to me in larger share ;
And in the third, so prospered was my stand,
That more new suits were entered by my hand
Than any other advocate could boast,
While scarcely one among them all was lost.

But here it may be useful to digress,
And state the causes of such rare success.

I looked on lawyers as a special class
Of men, raised high above the common mass,
That justice might be ministered to all,
Alike to rich and poor, to great and small,
With an impartial, firm, and potent voice,
In which all honest hearts should still rejoice.

This class I held to be the growth alone
Of Christianity.   It was not known
In Rome or Greece, until the Gospel rose
To shed its light upon its heathen foes.
It was not known amongst old Israel's race;
And now it is not found in any place
Throughout the world, save only where the Word
Of Christian truth pays homage to the Lord.

The class of lawyers who, of yore, had come
To great importance in imperial Rome,
Sunk quite away through Europe in the age
When Goths and Vandals occupied the stage.
The little learning then for centuries found
Was only seen within the Church's ground.
And when we next discern the lawyers' art,
It was the clergy who performed their part;
Thus clearly proving their belief to be,
That law and Gospel always should agree.

The fifteenth century produced a change:
Learning revived, and took a wider range;
The clergy left the law to other tongues,
Reserving all that to the soul belongs;
But still remained the plain and sacred sign
Which binds the lawyer to the rule divine.

For, first, he holds his license from the Court

To which the whole community resort
For justice.   And no case can there be tried
Until religion's seal has been applied.
The oath to God is taken by them all.
The judge, the jury, on the Lord must call;
The lawyers and the witnesses must swear
Their strict resolve to do their duty there.
And thus the bond of Christian faith we find
Distinctly placed, in form, on every mind.
From this plain proof no skeptic can withdraw,
'T is "part and parcel" of the Common Law.

I next reflected that 't was here alone
The oath of office o'er the work was thrown.
The Doctors, Teachers, Artists, Men of Trade,
Are under no such obligation laid.
The Manufacturers, though hundreds live
Beneath their influence, no such pledges give.
The Generals in the army, though a host
Of men may by their negligence be lost;
The Admirals, on whom it may depend
The welfare of the nation to defend;
In fine, the vast varieties of life
Which form this world of labor and of strife
Are all allowed to enter on their course
Without an oath their duty to enforce.
In this, the work of Justice stands apart;
The oath of office guards the lawyer's art:

And here Religion must exert her sway,
To be the safe director of his way.

And rightly !   To the strength of law we owe
The best security of all below.
Before the law, all human power should bow,
With trustful feeling and submissive brow.
From law alone each citizen expects
The rule which every social right protects.
'T is law which forces villainy to cease.
'T is law which guards our property in peace.
It is the majesty of law which spreads
Its sacred ægis over all our heads,
Forbidding tyrant force, led on by pride,
In triumph o'er our liberty to ride ;
Forbidding fraud, with mean and venal art,
To act successfully its treacherous part ;
And still dispensing, with its sovereign hand,
The light of truth and justice through the land.

But what is law ?   A rule of action given,
At first, by the authority of Heaven.
God gave His law in Paradise, that so
The happy tenants might their duty know.
He gave His law to Noah, and in fine,
Proclaimed through Moses' lips a Code divine.
The Ten Commands which from Mount Sinai came
In clouds of darkness lit by lightning's flame,

Were uttered by His voice who reigns on high
The Sovereign Master of the earth and sky.
The moral law, by His creative art,
Is written in the conscience of each heart ;
And thus, through all the heathen world, the
       ground
Of that great law in every race is found.
But Christian nations have it full and clear,
For, in the Written Word, its rules appear
In all their force.   From these our laws descend :
By these their sanctity we can defend,
In all the catalogue of grievous crime
And rights of property.   'T is true that time
Has introduced some other laws, whose claim
To veneration cannot be the same ;
Yet even to these the law of Christ applies,
When the Apostle's words before us rise :
" Submit to every ordinance of man
For conscience' sake."   Such is the Gospel plan ;
And thus obedience to the law's control
Is bound by power divine upon the soul.

Hence to my mind it seemed so plain and clear
That all the work of law should close adhere
To Christian duty.   Hence the oath which binds
The lawyer's conscience in good reason finds
An ample warrant for its high appeal
To God, the Lawgiver, that men may feel

Their true allegiance to His power, and still
Make known their reverence for His sacred will :
Since otherwise, that solemn oath must be
An awful mocking of His majesty.
The reckless man that takes it in such guise
Begins his course in blasphemy and lies,
And just as sure as death and judgment come,
Brings down upon his head a fearful doom !

With views like these my legal course was run,
And much I fear I was the only one
That held them.   Save myself, no lawyer there
Professed the Christian faith, or seemed to care
For any rule superior to the scale
In which the morals of the world prevail.
And hence I found the leaders of the bar
Disposed to carry on a sort of war
On my religion.   They could not deny
That in sound argument I might defy
The best among them.   Hence they only spoke
As if my Christian garb was but a cloak
Of sheer hypocrisy, for sordid ends,
Designed to make all pious men my friends.
Thus they accounted for my rapid growth
In character and business, nothing loath,
On this poor ground, my whole success to brand,
And slander what they could not understand.

But this was not the favored course with all.
There were exceptions, neither few nor small,
Of younger lawyers, who, with generous will,
Approved my care, my talents, and my skill
With more applause than I presumed to claim,
And kindly helped to recommend my name.

The principles of practice I pursued
Were only meant for justice and for good.
I undertook no case till I was sure
My client's cause this test could well endure.
When he had told his story, 't was my plan
To ask him frankly how the other man
Had viewed the matter.   Thus I always tried
To see the ground of difference on each side ;
And if it were a case of oral proof,
That I from all mistake might stand aloof,
I made him bring his witnesses, and so
The truth from their own statement I could know.
Then, if a doubt remained, it was my part
To recommend a compromise.   No art
Which I could use would save him from a train
Of cost and contest, all perhaps in vain.
'T was better for his pocket and his peace
From litigation's plagues and toils to cease,
Than seek a dubious game at law to play,
Where time and money might be thrown away.

By such a course I rarely failed to find
My clients willing to adopt my mind.
But if, as sometimes happened, they were bent
On legal contest, they had my consent
To try some other lawyer.   On the ground
Which I believed to be correct and sound
I could not offer to become their guide
Unless I had plain justice on my side.
If, by my client's statement, I could see
His cause was one of great uncertainty,
I felt quite sure, had I the power to hear
His adversary, 't would much worse appear.
And so it proved.   When they would not embrace
The counsel I had given, they lost the case,
And came to me as soon as it was o'er,
With confidence far stronger than before.

In all the legal business of that day
The clients suffered by the law's delay ;
But here, I had good reason to suspect,
The evil was the fruit of sheer neglect.
In this too common fault I had no share.
No toil was spared my cases to prepare ;
No time was idly suffered to be lost,
Nor was there any waste of care and cost.
This habit, by degrees, well known became,
And aided greatly to advance my name.
In cases of collection suits for debt

I found that lawyers sometimes would forget
To pay their clients' money. No excuse
Could be admitted for this gross abuse.
But I was punctual to the very hour
Which placed the sums collected in my power,
Remitting them at once, with prompt good will,—
A duty I took pleasure to fulfil.

Yet, when compassion's counsels might prevail,
I shunned the misery of a sheriff's sale.
If the poor debtor's friends could well secure
The final payment, so that this was sure,
I took all pains the case to represent,
And gain my worthy client's free consent
To give him ample time, with patience due,
And save his property and credit too.
The thanks which I received in this regard
Were felt to be a full and rich reward.

And there was still another pleasing part
In which I often worked with all my heart.
Whene'er my client's case seemed to admit
Of peaceful compromise, I deemed it fit
To bring the parties to my office, there
To listen to their statements, and compare
The plain advantage, if they could agree,
With all the plague and contest which must be
The fruit of litigation. Many a strife

Was thus composed within my legal life
To mutual satisfaction.   'T was my end
To act at once as lawyer and as friend ;
And though in such a work my fees were small,
The good resulting paid me for it all !

But in my new vocation I was taught
The vast advantage of the knowledge brought
From all my previous labors.   Sooth to say,
At first I deemed those years were thrown away.
Yet now I found the wide experience gained
In men and general business well sustained
My legal duties.   Hence my mind could claim
More sympathy with every class that came
For consultation.   Hence the tribes of trade,
Mechanics, merchants, farmers, all were made
To feel at ease in telling me their case,
As they perceived how well I could embrace
Their several interests.   And when the day
Of trial came, the same advantage lay
With witnesses.   Besides, I could command
More skill to make the jury understand
The bearing of the evidence, and reach
The art to fix attention to my speech.
The general information I possessed
Was thus full oft with good effect expressed.
" Knowledge is power," and those who have it can
Use the best influence of man on man.

The principles on which my practice grew,
Religion showed me, were correct and true.
'T was from the Bible that I sought to gain
The rule of life my labors to sustain.
Each morning summoned me and mine to pray
For grace and guidance through the passing day:
Each night beheld us at the sacred shrine,
To thank the Lord of truth and love divine.
And thus His blessing rested on the skill
Which moved in concord with His perfect will!

But while my rising prospects at the bar
My own most sanguine hopes surpassed by far,
And I was fully conscious that my name
Might yet be linked with fortune and with fame,
I often felt disgusted at the sight
Which legal strife exposes to the light, —
A mass of falsehood, meanness, fraud, and crime !
And then I longed to consecrate my time
To that more sacred ministry of love
Which advocates the wisdom from above,
And pleads to a condemned and sinful race
The Saviour's cause of mercy and of grace.
Especially on Sundays, when I saw
How much the pulpit sunk below the law
In zeal and talent.   We had lost the man
With whom my sacramental course began ;
And our small Church had suffered, year by year,

With preaching neither eloquent nor clear.
And as I listened to the poor display,
I wished, if possible, to find my way
To that great office, by whose pure control
I might promote the welfare of the soul.

This change, however, could not be, while yet
I lay beneath a heavy load of debt
To my late partner.　He had passed away,
And now his heirs possessed the legal sway
Of all his wealth.　But though they were to me
Indulgent friends, as kind as they could be,
I had no moral right to turn aside
From a profession which so well supplied
The means by which I still might hope to claim,
In time, my freedom from a debtor's name.
Besides, my children were a growing stock,
Two precious boys were added to my flock;
And so the thoughts of ministerial life
Must be postponed, and years of legal strife
Must be continued with a constant mind,
Until I could an honest warrant find.
But this, I felt, would be accomplished still,
If 't were so ordered by my Master's will.

About this time I had made up my mind
That my Freemasonry should be resigned.
For I, before my entrance at the bar,

Had joined the Lodge, and then gone on as far
As was consistent with the third degree.
That institution always seemed to me
Designed to foster moral truth and love;
Nor could I see good cause to disapprove
The law by which the just Freemason trod
A path commanded in the Word of God.
His square and compass were full well displayed,
With sacred reverence on the Bible laid;
His solemn oath, in language strong and plain,
Was always on that Holy Volume ta'en;
His contributions, regular and sure,
Were given to brethren, sick, or old, or poor;
Nor, when to estimate his rules I came,
Could I find aught to censure or to blame.
But still I thought consistency required
That the same Bible, thus in part admired,
Should be adopted, in its full control,
O'er all that regulates the life and soul.
On their own principles, Freemasons all
Should with true faith on their Redeemer call.
The Lodge, however fair its partial ground,
Can for the Church no substitute be found;
And yet, how many members there I saw
Resolved the false conclusion thus to draw,
Content to make the Lodge their only guide,
And caring nothing for all else beside !

From great King Solomon, as all suppose,
The noble Order of Freemasons rose ;
And Solomon possessed a mighty mind,
But he was not the Saviour of mankind.
Though wise as any mortal man could be,
Yet did he play the fool egregiously,
And sinned beyond the guilt of many lives,
By building heathen altars for his wives,
Instead of teaching them the Sacred Word,
And leading them in faith to serve the Lord.
By this most shameful conduct he brought down
A judgment on the nation.   Union gone !
Ten tribes revolted !   Israel's peace had fled,
And war intestine raised its horrid head.
No art the former Union could restore,
And all their boasted greatness was no more !

Three books of Solomon, it is most true,
Attributed to inspiration due,
Have always by the Church admitted been.
But in these writings not one word is seen
About the founding of an Order new,
Who should the work of Masonry pursue.
Josephus, the historian of the Jews,
Thought fit such information to refuse.
And not one scrap of evidence appears,
Through all the records of two thousand years,
Until the Middle Ages.   There we meet

With facts of much significance, to greet
The eyes of the explorer.   When the sword
Of the Crusaders triumphed o'er the horde
Of Saracens, and Baldwin took the throne
In old Jerusalem, a work was done
Which well might seem, with reason good, to be
The worthy source of this fraternity.
For then a Temple was rebuilt with care,
And Knightly orders rose, with purpose fair,
To guard the Christian pilgrims from the foe ;
While all the builders, that the world might know
Their grand achievement, formed an Order too,
And from that time their art in honor grew :
Thence the Masonic Brotherhood came down
From age to age, with credit and renown.

To this fair theory I gave my mind,
Because no other method I could find
By which to reconcile Masonic acts
With the historic evidence of facts.
The building of this Temple would suggest
The work of Solomon, and all the rest
Which in the Scripture narrative we see,
As obvious points of true analogy ;
But there was nothing which I heard or knew
To indicate the system of the Jew ;
While there were two great matters, clear and
          plain,
Which nought except the Gospel could explain.

First, that the square and compass were displayed
On the whole Bible, therefore they were laid
On the *New Testament:* the Special Word,
Which leads us to our Saviour as THE LORD.
Next, that the Festal day in all the year
Is taken from the Gospel.   This is clear.
In concord with the Knights of good St. John,
His day was ever chosen as the one
Which all Freemasons honor with a zeal
Becoming faithful Christian men to feel.
Now these are facts no argument can bring
Within the times of Israel's Jewish king.
The common notion, as it seemed to me,
Had neither proof nor probability.
I had no doubt the first Freemasons were,
As true believers, men of faith and prayer,
Belonging to the Church in deed and name,
And their successors still should be the same.

A further evidence of this was shown
From facts of history to all men known.
For since the time when Rome's triumphant sway
Had driven the Jews from their own land away,
For fifteen centuries and more, their place,
Through Europe, was a by-word of disgrace;
And no Society which claimed its power
From Jewish sources could have lived an hour
Amongst a Christian people.   This, to me,

Seemed proof as positive as proof could be ;
Nor could my mind, regarded in this shape,
In any mode from the result escape.

But the majority were fixed.   With them,
No argument the prejudice could stem.
And hence it soon became my strong desire
With all respect and kindness to retire.
And so I took my leave in form.   Since then
I never visited the Lodge again.

Canto Seventh.

HE time now came when constant labor
brought
A fearful warning to the powers of
thought.
Too much employment in official care,
Too little exercise in open air ; —
My brain began to suffer, and the range
Of daily toil required a thorough change.

One night, preparing to retire to bed,
A strange sensation struck upon my head.
No language can describe the kind of pain.
I felt convinced that I should be insane
If it continued.   So at once I ran
To my physician's home, — that same kind man
Who had been warning me, for years before,
That my career on earth must soon be o'er,
Unless my constant labors were combined
With healthful relaxation to my mind.
The dose of paregoric which he gave
Relieved my nerves, and I resolved to brave

My friend's advice no longer. The next day
I bought an out-lot near two miles away ;
And in brief time I built a dwelling there,
That I my weakened strength might thus repair
By wholesome exercise ; and then I took,
As junior partner, one who well could look
After the office. He had studied law,
And all my mode of practice clearly saw,
As inmate of my family full long, —
By Nature gifted with a judgment strong,
And well adapted to perform his part
With careful energy and skilful art.

My constitution soon regained its strength,
And I, to please my clients, went at length,
Though with reluctance, some few days to spend,
A neighboring Court in term-time to attend.
And while contending there in legal strife
The fact took place which changed my future life,
And gave that life, by Heaven's divine control,
To the great work which long possessed my soul.

Amongst the vestrymen that held the care
Of our small church, I had a friend who there
Possessed the influence which honest zeal
Inclines the hearts of Christian men to feel.
To him I had conveyed, one year before,
The inclination which my judgment bore

6

Towards the vocation by the Lord designed
To be the guide and teacher of mankind,
Ready in this my service to display
Whenever He should please to ope the way.

No further conference between us passed
Upon the subject; but I found, at last,
That he on this foundation laid a plan,
Without my knowledge, and his work began
While I was absent.   Word was sent to all
To hold a parish meeting, and to call
Another pastor; for the church had then
Beheld for months a vacant desk again,
And our last minister had failed to prove
An object either of respect or love.
A goodly number to the meeting came,
And then my zealous friend proposed my name
As future rector, if I were agreed
To give up my profession, and proceed
As soon as possible to be ordained:
The service of the Church to be sustained
By me as their Lay Reader, till the hour
When I could act with ministerial power.

My friend then told them that he knew my mind
Had long been strongly to this work inclined.
'T was true the sacrifice which I must make
Was large.   I should be called on to forsake

A prosperous business, greater now, by far,
Than many lawyers at the Pittsburgh bar.
My income on an average must be clear
Four or five thousand dollars every year,
While as their rector I could not control
More than a poor eight hundred on the whole.
And he had no authority from me
To say as yet what the result might be ;
But still he trusted to the ardent zeal
Which for the Church he thought my heart must
      feel,
And urged his hearers that they ought to ask
My free consent to undertake the task,
In hope to make my resolution sure,
And thus my life-long labor to secure.

This proposition was so new and strange
That it produced a wide and varied range
Of warm discussion.   Yet, as I was told,
No speaker on the subject seemed to hold
A doubt that I was qualified to fill
The sacred office, if I had the will.
The loss of income was the only ground
On which objection to the plan was found.
But all dispute was yielded in the end.
The resolution offered by my friend
Was in due form propounded at the last,
And with unanimous concurrence passed.

On my return, this parish act was laid
Before my eyes, and the impression made
Exceeds all power of language to express;
For in my business I had great success.
If in that noble calling I should stay,
Fortune and honor full before me lay;
While, in the ministry, the paltry gain
Could not my precious family sustain.
Three hundred dollars must be paid beside,
Which, year by year, my mother's wants supplied;
And that annuity the sacred law
Of filial love forbade me to withdraw.
Moreover, there was still the heavy debt
To my late partner's heirs, which must be met;
And how, with all those claims upon my hand,
Could I in poverty expect to stand?
Under these circumstances it was clear
That such a change mere madness must appear;
And worldly prudence seemed at once to show
The only course in which I ought to go.

But then, had I not here received a call
Of highest duty from the Lord of all? —
A call like which no other case was known,
In form peculiar, strange, and quite alone? —
A call whose only theory could be,
That it was ordered by His wise decree?
Had not His Holy Spirit drawn my will,

For years, this sacred function to fulfil
Whene'er the hand of God should lead the way,
And should I now that high resolve betray?
Grant that a host of worldly fears and cares
Might spring around me, with their specious
       snares,
Could I not trust His goodness who had shed
So many gracious blessings on my head?
Nay, was there not a special promise given
To those who left their earthly gain for Heaven?
And would not every sacrifice, so made,
By His munificence be well repaid?

But still my former partner's heirs possessed
A right which could not justly be repressed;
And hence I went to them without delay,
Submitting to their will what I should say.
For they were Christians who could understand
The rule which my decision should command,
And thus their judgment might afford a clue
To guide me in the path I should pursue.

The gracious answer from these friends received
My mind from its chief doubt at once relieved.
That debt, they said, should never bar the way.
The dictates of my heart I must obey;
Nor would they e'er presume to hold a rod
Of legal justice o'er a call from God!

The path seemed open now, for well I knew
The feelings of my precious wife were true.
No fear of want or trouble could appall
Her pious confidence.   She hailed my call
With grateful pleasure, longing for the hour
When I could use my undivided power
To serve that glorious Lord whose hand divine
So long had kindly guarded me and mine.

My mind at length made up, with faith and
          prayer,
I went to Philadelphia to prepare
My way to Ordination.   Here I found,
From Bishop, Clergy, Laity, a round
Of cordial welcome.   When that work was done,
Lay reading in the church at once begun ;
And from that hour my humble labors bore
An interest never witnessed there before.

For many years their organ I had played ;
And now my faithful wife, though much afraid,
Assumed the post.   To make her task more plain,
I wrote her voluntaries, and the strain
Which served as interlude to every verse ;
And those each week she could at home rehearse.
Thus for four years she occupied the ground,
Until another organist was found.

My care was next my business to dispose,
That I at once my lawyer's life might close ;
And here the opportunity was given,
By the still favoring Providence of Heaven.

The able Henry Baldwin held a name
Of high preëminence in legal fame ;
And now, four years in Congress being passed,
He deemed it prudent to return at last
To his profession.   That he might secure
My business, which he knew was large and sure,
He made an offer, liberal and fair,
To my young colleague, that they both should
        share
As partners, if I would transfer the whole
To them, so far as I possessed control,
For a just price.   I was rejoiced to find
That I could thus so soon relieve my mind
From a great burden.   The amount to state,
My youthful partner made the estimate,
And found, that, from the cases then in train,
Twelve thousand dollars ought to be the gain.
On this they offered me, in notes of hand,
Three thousand only.   But I would not stand
To argue on the terms.   The deed was done !
My final cause was pleaded, and was won.
The eighth day of November saw me free ;
The year was eighteen hundred twenty-three.

The next December, on the fourteenth day,
Invited by the Bishop to display
My office as a Deacon, just conferred.
The congregation of St. Peter's heard
My first discourse.   And when, in May, I came
To the Convention, they allowed my claim
To be ordained a Priest, — a rapid race
From legal practice to a Rector's place!

The reasons for this hasty course were two,
And some attention to them both seems due.

For many years ere the result was seen,
The Bible had my daily study been.
And while I practised law, each night some part
Of the Greek Testament was laid to heart.
The Latin Classics had not lost their power;
With Cicero and Horace many an hour
Was spent with pleasure: but the larger share
Of time and thought, with close attentive care,
Was given to Church Theology.   The lore
Of Pearson, Hooker, Burnet, was a store
From which religion could a system draw:
Grotius and Paley, Stillingfleet and Law,
Bingham and Mosheim, also had a claim,
With many others whom I need not name:
So that the learning was already gained,
And on that score my care was well sustained.

The second reason for such quick despatch
Was this. They deemed it wisdom to attach
A high importance to the act which led
The Protestant Church to choose me for its
    head.
West of the Alleghanies, in that day,
No other Church of our Communion lay.
The Bishop was a sight as yet unseen:
Across the mountains he had never been.
No clergyman was near, his aid to lend. —
On me alone the service must depend.
Hence for the Church's sake, much more than
    mine,
The time was shortened with the best design.

The change of my profession had produced
A strong sensation. Many tongues were loosed
In censure of my folly, thus to yield
A certain fortune in the legal field:
While others praised the fervent, honest zeal
Which by that act 't was certain I must feel.
The interest thus created told with force
Upon the Church. A bright and prosperous
    course
Began forthwith, and in the month of May
My kind Masonic brethren came to lay
The corner-stone of our new building, planned
In Gothic beauty, by the sexton's hand. —

The first attempt throughout our country known,
Which had that style of architecture shown.
The congregation rapidly increased,
And in the following year we had a feast
Of pure enjoyment, when the Bishop came
To consecrate our Church, and grant the claim
Of full one hundred forty-three to pay
Their vows in Confirmation on that day.
The venerable prelate, Bishop White,
And Reverend Jackson Kemper, hailed the sight,
So far beyond what the most sanguine mind
Could hope so soon in our new field to find;
While I, with feelings words cannot express,
Thanked God who thus my work had deigned to
      bless.

Our dwelling still continued on the lot
Of ten fair acres. 'T was a lovely spot,
Where I had built a modest house of frame,
Planted an orchard of the choicest name,
Set out a garden, and, to guard the ground,
Made a young hedge of evergreen around.
Three other lots I bought, of equal size,
Which proved to be a most important prize;
For they were offered at so little cost
That in the purchase nothing could be lost,
And in few years the value rose so high,
That by their sale I could the means supply

To pay my partner's heirs that heavy debt.
Their generous faith, which I can ne'er forget,
Made this a grateful duty, in the hour
When the good Lord thus placed it in my power.
And 't was a duty done with praise to Heaven,
Whose Providence the privilege had given
With much less toil and in less time by far
Than if I had continued at the bar : —
A proof how surely sacrifices, made
With love to Christ, are even here o'erpaid ;
While blessings manifold are granted still,
To those who humbly strive to do His will !

But I, meanwhile, before this point was gained,
Commenced a school by which I was sustained :
For though my rector's salary had grown
To full twelve hundred dollars, yet 't was known
That this could not accomplish the design
To feed and clothe a family like mine.
My precious wife had added to our stock
Two children more.   It was a growing flock.
And we embraced the offer of a friend,
Six little girls without delay to send
For education, with our own to live,
And share the home instruction we could give.

The school which thus so quietly begun,
Was destined soon a prosperous course to run.

My buildings were enlarged.   A separate band
Of boys were placed beneath my ruling hand.
A student of Theology became
Their teacher; and a young but steady dame,
Accustomed to the task, performed her share,
For all the girls committed to my care.
Two schools distinct in each department grew
From this beginning.   'T was an effort new,
And brought of daily toil a heavy load;
Yet both were favored by the love of God.
We had our little Oratory there,
With organ, kept for morn and evening prayer;
Once in each week, with all my care and skill,
I taught my schools to know their Saviour's will;
And had the blessed office to impart
His living faith to many a youthful heart!

Seven years of happy labor thus were spent,
With rich results of comfort and content.
The burden of such varied, busy life,
At times bore hardly on my faithful wife;
Our toil was unremitting and severe,
But order, peace, and love were round us there!

Yet though my time was thus absorbed, I found
The means to plant the Church on other ground.
Seven parishes were organized, and gained

A foothold which has since been well sustained;
And seven young candidates around me came,
Moved to assume the ministerial name.
With zealous will they studied at my side,
And I was happy to be called their guide.

Canto Eighth.

SOON after my new course was well begun,
I saw, with pain, how party lines had run
Amongst my brethren, tending to divide
Good faithful clergymen on either side.
High Church and Low contended with a zeal
Of strong repulsion which I could not feel,
For I expected in the Church to prove
Naught but fraternal unity and love.

But both the parties were disposed to be
Quite cordial in their intercourse with me.
Low Churchmen were well satisfied to find
My mode of preaching suited to their mind.
High Churchmen were contented when they saw
That I was true to order and to law.
My vows of ordination bound me still
In fair obedience to my Bishop's will.
I had a great advantage in the war
Of words, from my long training at the bar.

This, with the lawyers, gave a special claim,
And thus a general favorite I became;
For, still desirous that all strife should cease,
I used my powers for concord and for peace.

The venerated Bishop White had now,
Beneath his eighty years, begun to bow,
And asked for an Assistant, who might bear
Of active work the more laborious share.
This measure roused the fire of party zeal,
With which no moderate man could wisely deal.
But the Convention failed to make a choice;
The votes were balanced with an equal voice:
And then my High-Church brethren turned to
      me,
Resolved that I their candidate should be.

This notion struck my mind with great surprise.
The office of a Bishop, in my eyes,
Required experience, knowledge, skill to teach,
In a degree which I might never reach.
I was a novice; scarce had passed away
Three busy years since that most solemn day
When I received the priesthood. How could I
The work of the Episcopate supply?

Our next Convention season now drew near,
Which called us all in order to appear.

My friends in caucus met: the work began,
By casting ballots for their favorite man;
And I had all the votes save three alone,
Elected thus to be the chosen one.
Nothing was wanting but my own consent,
And that I could not give.   With frank intent,
I told my brethren why I did not deem
That such a choice would wise or prudent
    seem,
But pledged my vote for any other name
Which their support and Bishop White's could `
    claim ;
Since I the clergy had too little known,
To have a settled judgment of my own.

On this I left the meeting, with my breast
Most deeply by this proof of love impressed.
When I retired, it was resolved, at length,
For Doctor Onderdonk to use their strength.
Meanwhile, my Low-Church brethren too had
    met,
And chose no candidate.   But they were set,
With their united efforts to oppose
The person whom the other party chose ;
And on the morrow, when the House agreed
That the election should at once proceed,
They pleaded zealously, with all their power,
For a recess, if only for an hour,

That, after friendly conference, they might
Choose one in whom both parties could unite.

During the progress of this strange dispute
I sat apart, much moved, but wholly mute ;
Though several brethren from the Low-Church
    side
Came round, and for my help with warmth
    applied.
" Get us this conference," they said, " and you
Will be our Bishop." I replied, " 'T is due,
On every principle of Christian love
And Christian courtesy. If you could prove
That *my* election was not in your mind,
I should at once be to the task inclined.
But now the very reason you declare
Compels me to be silent. To the care
Of such high office I do not aspire ;
I am not fit, nor should I dare desire
In that result to bear the slightest part,
Though for your wish I thank you from my
    heart."

The plea for conference was all in vain.
The High-Church party firmly held the rein.
They had a bare majority of one
Among the clergy, hence my vote alone
Elected Doctor Onderdonk. But lo !

7

The other party were resolved to show
That in my favor they had really striven,
Since for my name full seventeen votes were
    given !
The record thus presents a curious state ;
For I appear the Low-Church candidate,
Though chosen in caucus by the High-Church
    side
Till I, in conscience, my consent denied.
The office was entirely in my power,
And I feel humbly grateful, to this hour,
That I was strengthened, by the grace divine,
A charge so grave and weighty to decline.

Soon after this event, an offer came,
Commended by good Bishop Hobart's name,
In great New York, the rector to become
Of old St. Stephen's.   To my cherished home
A special member of the Vestry brought
The formal call, and I was much besought,
In many letters, to accept the post ;
But I declined it, though I had a host
Of friends amongst the clergy, good and true,
With much kind favor from the Bishop too, —
That generous-hearted prelate, who had gained
A wide-spread influence, by few attained.

The Presbyterians, that important sect, —

In Pittsburgh held so long in high respect, —
Had now, to strengthen their religious rule,
Resolved to build a Theologic school;
And I, with thought and prayer, at once began
To form a fair and practicable plan,
Which might, on a foundation firm and sure,
For our dear Church a like result secure.
With this intent I set apart a lot
Of full three acres, a commanding spot,
O'erlooking the Ohio, near the road,
Precisely opposite to my abode.
This, estimated by a standard fair,
Would make three thousand dollars for my share.
Two thousand more were promised by a few,
Who were persuaded to adopt my view;
And no one doubted of a prosperous end,
If the Convention would the plan commend.

Before that body the design was laid,
And, judging by the kindly speeches made,
They would at once have with my offer closed,
But Bishop Onderdonk was quite opposed.
He thought the Seminary at New York
Was all sufficient for the Church's work.
And though they voted to commit the case
To the next meeting, yet, to run a race
Against my Bishop's judgment, seemed to me
A course with which my mind could not agree;

My hopes were thus effectually crossed,
And I regarded all this labor lost.

The Church of Trinity, in Boston, next
Gave me an urgent call, which much perplexed
My Vestry, for they now began to fear
That my departure must be drawing near.
With warmth they begged me promptly to decline;
And this I did, for I had no design
To leave my cherished parish ere the day
When duty's voice should summon me away.

The Rector of that church in Boston, then,
Was one beyond the average of men,
Distinguished by his talents and his fame,
The Reverend Mr. Doane.   The call which came
Was to be his assistant ; but 't was placed
On a peculiar fund, and fitly graced
By a much larger salary.   His zeal
To have my aid persuaded me to feel
That there was more than common in the field,
And made me sometimes half inclined to yield.
He wrote in answer, warmly to request
That I would visit him, and take my rest
At least two Sundays, even if my will
To stay in Pittsburgh should continue still.
My Vestry thought it right that I should go,
This act of kindly courtesy to show ;

While neither they nor I could apprehend
The undesired and unexpected end.

Arrived in Boston, at the Rector's home,
I found that I had now in truth become
A sort of lion, feasted and caressed,
With all the welcome that could be expressed.
But chiefly, in our private talks alone,
The need of aid to lower the proud tone
Of Unitarian heresy, was held
Before my eyes, by honest warmth impelled :
For this was there supreme, and chained the mind
Of the best educated and refined.
Channing still lived, and with his winning art
Dazzled the intellect and charmed the heart ;
And if I would the Church's banner bear,
Where most 't was needed, I should labor there.

My Seminary scheme he next discussed,
And said, that, if to him I would intrust
The office, he would carry out my plan
For Massachusetts.   In no other man
Were both the parties willing to unite ;
But High and Low believed my course was right.
· Both would have made me Bishop if they could,
And both would aid me in a work so good.
'T was true the post to which I had the call
Appeared subordinate, but that was all.

In point of fact, as could be clearly shown,
It was as independent as his own.
The salary was larger, and the task
Which he and the proprietors would ask
Should be to half the public service tied;
The prayer and preaching we should both divide.
No parish labor would be claimed from me,
And through the week-days I should thus be
     free
The duties of Professor to fulfil,
And guide the Seminary at my will.

These views, with kind and cordial warmth ex-
     pressed,
Made a profound impression on my breast.
Nor did the friendly Rector fail to claim
That many other brethren held the same.
For soon he had a sumptuous banquet set,
Where I, the Bishop, and the Clergy met;
And all I heard contributed its share
My mind for this new movement to prepare.

But here it may be useful to explain
The course that led my wishes to attain
The founding of a Theologic school,
Conducted on the old patristic rule,
Where students might be trained in all the lore
Which our Reformers mastered long before,

Instead of wandering, full oft astray,
In modern Germany's delusive way,
And treating with neglect each weighty tome
Which bears upon the Church's strife with Rome.

At Pittsburgh, in those days, there chanced to be
A good Benevolent Society,
Composed of native Irishmen, whose aim
Was to assist the emigrants that came
To seek a refuge in our prosperous land,
And give them, in their need, a helping hand.
During the period when I practised law
I was their President, and often saw
The Roman priest, who, once a year at least,
Made his appearance at St. Patrick's feast, —
An Irishman of talent, growing gray,
But learned and eloquent, and sometimes gay.

When my career of law was fully run,
And ministerial work had well begun,
I thought that I would undertake a course
Of sermons on our Articles. The force
Of all our writers' arguments I knew,
And doubted not that they were just and true.
But now the legal rule occurred to me,
" Hear both the parties first, and then decree."
And I resolved the rule should be applied
By careful reading on the Romish side.

Father McGuire forthwith I went to find,
And quickly made him understand my mind.
He hailed my resolution with delight.
Perhaps I seemed a convert in his sight.
If so, it proved to be a slight mistake!
But he proceeded instantly to make
A good selection of nine quartos rare,
Composed by Jesuits, in Latin fair, —
A series of authorities as high
As any work in Europe could supply
Upon the controversy.   These, he said,
I might take home, and at my leisure tread
The path of Theologic truth and light,
With hope that I would firmly choose the right.
Thanking the kind old priest, I went my way,
And entered on my task without delay.

I found the Fathers quoted on their side,
And with much ingenuity applied,
The forms of logic used with skilful art,
While Scripture bore at times an honored part.
But from my habits in the school of law
I saw, with ease, full many a serious flaw.
And all that gave me trouble was to find
The seeming judgment of the Fathers' mind.
This led me to conclude that I must try
To read them for myself, and thus supply
A certain method to attain my end,
To combat error and the truth defend.

The work of Irenæus chanced to be
For sale. At once I bought it, glad to see
What from that martyr Bishop forth had gone,
In seventy years from the Apostle John.
With special joy I read the ancient page,
Which proved, that, in his pure and early age,
The Church knew nothing of the papal plan,
Whose lordly claims long afterwards began,
But made, throughout, the rule of faith accord
With the sole doctrine of the written Word !

Tertullian next, and Cyprian, I found
In Philadelphia. The patristic round
Was not completed, till, from year to year,
I had imported seventy volumes clear ;
Besides the Councils, Histories, Decrees, —
All proving through what changes, by degrees,
The Church of Rome had gained her mighty
          sway,
Resolved by fraud or force to win the day.

But from the first those studies had impressed
A deep and strong desire upon my breast
To found a school where this patristic lore
Should be regarded as the proper store
From which our clergy might well armed become
In all their conflicts with the Church of Rome.
My plan for Pennsylvania was foreclosed,

For Bishop Onderdonk stood there opposed.
And hence, when Massachusetts seemed inclined
To do the work according to my mind,
It looked to me as if the favoring hand
Of Providence had pointed out the land
Where I could labor with the fullest scope
For all my industry, in faith and hope.
I saw that then, throughout the Church at large,
No man had ta'en this serious task in charge.
The controversies warmly carried on
Were with the sects of Protestants alone ;
While the great controversy, on whose ground
Our right to Reformation could be found,
Appeared so settled, that no thought nor care
Was needed for that conflict to prepare.
And yet the power of Rome was growing fast,
For shoals of Roman Catholics were cast
From Europe, year by year, upon our shore,
As time went on, increasing more and more.
The day was coming when that Church would
        stand,
A proud and potent agent in our land.
The Reformation battle, in my view,
We might be shortly called on to renew ;
And I, for one, would gird me for the fight,
Prepared to prove our English martyrs right.
And hence I longed for the Professor's name,
That others might be trained to do the same.

This duty, which had long possessed my mind,
Now made me feel to Boston much inclined.
Although it would remove me far away
From Pittsburgh, where my warm affections lay
Although no other home could e'er impart
Such feelings of attachment to my heart ;
Although I knew the change would sorely grieve
The host of partial friends whom I must leave,
And be a source of sorrow to that wife
Who was the dearest treasure of my life :
Yet duty to the Master whom I served
My resolution to the effort nerved.
'T was but a little sacrifice to make
To Him who died for His dear Church's sake !

I told the cordial Rector, ere I went,
That I to take his offer was content,
If their Convention, which was soon to meet,
His plan by their full sanction should complete :
And so proceeded to my much-loved home,
Destined, ere long, another's to become,
With my dear partner talked the matter o'er,
And found her ever ready, as of yore,
To yield her feelings, hopefully resigned,
In faithful concord with her husband's mind.

The letter came full soon. The work was done !
The Rector's triumph was completely won !

The vote of the Convention fixed the plan,
And now my painful task of change began.
My resignation of the parish proved
How well and deeply I had been beloved!
My scholars were disbanded, all around
The voice of grief and sad regret I found.
My wife's dear family were sore distressed.
Her precious sister's heart was most oppressed;
For she with us had long possessed a home,
And her society had thus become
A cherished feature, felt with kindly force
Throughout the circle of our wedded course.
Her Christian temper, and her constant aim
To serve and profit all who near her came,
Made her a treasure!   But she could not stay,
And leave her honored parents far away.
For they were aged, and had none beside
By whom a daughter's care could be supplied.
With her the parting had most bitter been;
Two sisters so attached were rarely seen!

At length 't was settled.   House and goods were
        sold,
And I left Pittsburgh, rich enough in gold,
More rich in family and cordial love!
A brighter lot few mortal men could prove.
But 't was a sacrifice of feeling deep,
And strong emotion would full often sweep

Across our breasts, when we surveyed the ground,
Where we such labors and such joys had found.
Eight children now our married life had graced :
One lovely boy was in the church-yard placed ;
The rest went with us to our new abode,
And on them all the hand of God bestowed
A well-formed body and an active mind,
Which seemed to duty and to truth inclined.
And we had left of friends a cordial band,
A residence erected by my hand,
Orchard and gardens planted by my care,
And, above all, that precious House of Prayer,
Built in accordance with my own design,
Where I, for years, had preached the Word divine,
And furnished all the music for the choir, —
Chants, anthems, psalms, and hymns, at the desire
Of Organist and Vestry, while the roll
Which came beneath my pastoral control
In faith to share the Eucharistic feast
From thirty-seven to hundreds had increased !

And could we leave them all without a thrill
Of pain and sorrow ?   Could I hope to fill
Another phase of ministerial life
So rich in honor, so exempt from strife ?
Could other friends, howe'er disposed, impart
Such cordial love and comfort to my heart ?
Alas ! 't was more than doubtful.   But the Lord

Would still direct me by His sovereign Word;
His grace and truth would guide my future way,
Nor suffer me or mine to go astray.
Looking to Him all doubt should disappear:
Trusting in Him, what danger could I fear?

Canto Ninth.

UR tedious and expensive journey past,
We came to Boston safe and well at
last.
Our welcome there was gracious, warm, and kind.
I bought a house near Cambridge, to our mind,
By no means equal to our former home,
And yet a dwelling which might well become
Our new position.   Here six students met;
And I, as their Professor, duly set
Their lessons in Theology.   The rest
Was undertaken, with a cordial zest,
By Doctors Coit and Eaton, men of note,
And joint Professors by a formal vote.
Thus the good work, so long desired by me,
With prospects fair commenced now seemed to be.

As preacher I could ask no higher place.
The favor of my friends advanced apace:
My services were sought for, far and near,
And everything concurred my heart to cheer.
But time was ripening for a new display,
Which took me from my Boston friends away.

The Eastern diocese had ta'en its stand
Under the pious Bishop Griswold's hand,
For twenty years uniting as a whole,
To share his wise Episcopal control.
The churches in Vermont, New Hampshire,
        Maine,
Rhode Island, Massachusetts, formed a chain
Of mutual connection, while the name
Of diocese in each remained the same,
And each convened in every year to send
Its delegates the Council to attend.

It was in eighteen hundred thirty-one,
The month July, when my new work begun ;
And in September they assembled all,
In prompt compliance with the annual call.
'T was then Vermont her application set
Before the body in Convention met,
That, as she had in strength and numbers grown,
She might elect a Bishop of her own ;
She asked permission therefore to withdraw,
In due obedience to the Church's law.

To thwart this application none were bent ;
At once they granted it with full consent,
And in the month of May Vermont went on
To choose her Bishop. Reverend Doctor Stone
Was named by brethren on the Low-Church side ;

The other party all their zeal applied
To have that sacred office filled by me,
And triumphed by a bare majority.
In fact, the forces were so nearly even,
The ballots showed a vote of six to seven ;
But the minority, with Christian grace,
Agreed to give me my appointed place.
By letter they united in the call,
And signed the testimonials one and all ;
Thus seeming quite unanimous to prove
That they would welcome me with zeal and love.

This new announcement could not fail to throw
My mind in much perplexity. To go
From Boston, where the Lord had deigned to
        bless
My humble labors with so much success ;
To leave a circle of admiring friends,
For doubtful prospects and uncertain ends ;
My home just settled to break up again,
With toil and trouble, not unmixed with pain,
And put my future efforts in a shape
From which, through life, I could have no escape :
All this was most distasteful.   My desire
Did not to the Episcopate aspire.
Though I the office could most highly prize,
It had no strong attraction in my eyes.
Its ancient powers no longer were sustained,

While its responsibilities remained;
And I would rather see its mantle thrown
On any other shoulders than my own.

But yet the path of duty must be trod.
Was this to be esteemed a call from God?
If so, I must obey it.   To decide
That point, my efforts now were all applied.
With constant prayer for guidance I would sound
The judgment of my brethren all around,
And thus with time and caution I would try
Some light for my decision to supply.

I found that all my friends were strongly set
Against Vermont.   But still the case was met
On personal motives, flattering to my fame,
And quite regardless of the Church's claim.
My talents, they were pleased to say, would be
Quite buried in Vermont society;
I ought to have a larger, better field,
Than any the Green Mountain State could yield.
If I remained, my prospects would be sure,
A far superior mitre to secure.
Good Bishop Griswold now was growing old;
The time was coming when they would be told
To give him an Assistant; then should I
Be chosen the sacred office to supply!
By this I saw, should I refuse the call,

It would be deemed ambition by them all, —
A laudable ambition in their view,
Yet such as no true Christian should pursue.
Such counsels had the contrary effect ;
I would not give them reason to suspect
That motives of mere vanity and pride
Could be admitted my resolve to guide,
And hence their mode of argument, though kind,
Made me to serve Vermont feel more inclined.

The Vestry of old Trinity had sent
A fair committee, who their efforts spent
With cordial zeal to keep me as their own ;
The Vestry of St. Paul's had also shown
A strong desire that I should not depart ;
And many a tongue, inspired by friendly heart,
Gave touching evidence each day to prove
How high I stood in their esteem and love.
And most devoutly thankful did I feel
For all those marks of kindliness and zeal !

But the good Rector took the other side,
And thought the call ought not to be denied.
In my own mind the founding of the school,
Which in the previous year had formed the rule
To lead me from my cherished Pittsburgh home,
Might well a valid reason now become
For my refusal.   But in this I found

My hopes had rested on no solid ground.
'T was clear the school was raised to bring me
      there,
While for the thing itself none seemed to care.
And when the Annual Convention met,
And silence on its claims the seal had set,
I saw the influence of his master-mind
Had to his views my brethren well inclined.
The Board of Trustees were required to lay
Their full report, on the Convention day,
Before the House. But this they had not done ;
The school was looked upon as dead and gone!
Then I determined, without more delay,
To see Vermont, and after that survey
Make my resolve, which should conclusive be,
And put an end to all uncertainty.

I took my tour with pleasure, side by side
With that most zealous friend, who had supplied,
For years, the church at Bellows Falls, — the
      same
Who bears the Bishop of New Hampshire's name.
A charming country met my artist eye ;
Its fair Green Mountains raised their summits
      high,
Its lovely vales in summer's wealth arrayed,
Its shining lakelets and its forest shade,
Its prosperous villages, its schools well filled

With pupils in the common branches skilled,
While large academies, with just display,
For two good Colleges prepared the way;
Its men intelligent, its women fair,
Adorned full oft with grace and beauty rare;
No quarter of the land that I had seen
Could to my task have more adapted been.
And I could answer for my precious wife,
That she had parted long from city life,
And for our children's sake, if not our own,
Preferred by far the country to the town.
Here, then, if I accepted, we might trace
The most attractive forms of Nature's face,
Nor could we hope elsewhere a home to gain
More fair than Burlington, on Lake Champlain!

Soon after I returned, my answer went
Accepting the appointment. Then I sent
My resignation of the office held
In Trinity, as I should be compelled
To leave them in October, for the soil
Where Providence had fixed my future toil.

Much indignation and regret were shown
When my determination was made known.
The Rector had the largest share of blame,
And censure's tongue with zeal denounced his
      name;

Because I would have willingly refused
The Bishopric, if he had only used
His power the Seminary to sustain,
And me as its Professor to retain.
Many severe and foolish things were said,
To heap reproach and fault upon his head.
But yet I doubt not that he was sincere ;
The course of duty to his mind was clear ;
And though it gave some sorrow to my breast,
'T was well, and wisely ordered for the best.

A new event, however, was at hand,
For he was called before the Church to stand
Elected Bishop of New Jersey.   Strange
That Trinity should thus be forced to change
Both of her ministers, and see them take
The same high office for the Saviour's sake !

The General Convention now was due,
October, eighteen hundred thirty-two,
In old St. Paul's, New York.   It was a sight,
When four new Bishops stood to claim the rite
Of consecration.   First elect, my name
Was first admitted.   Then Kentucky came ;
Ohio third ; and last, the list to close,
New Jersey's chosen candidate arose.
The aged Bishop White his hands had laid,
For the third time, on my unworthy head !

My own emotion I remember well,
But 't was a feeling which no tongue can tell;
Nor could the power of rhetoric impart
The awe and gratitude which filled my heart,
That I, so early, should be called to prove
Such weighty office through my Master's love !

My duty, next, was to prepare the way,
And seek my diocese without delay.

My wife's good father, in a ripe old age,
With Christian hope had left this earthly stage.
Her mother and her sister came to be
The cherished inmates of our family.
Another son was added to our stock,
And two young pupils still increased our flock.
Fourteen in all were thus to take the road
Which led to Burlington, our new abode.
A coach was chartered for our use alone,
And in November all that work was done.
St. Paul's new Church had just erected been,
And I was Rector. 'T was a novel scene,
In which, though toil and trouble had their share,
We proved the blessing of our Saviour's care.

My tour of visitation I went round.
A cordial welcome everywhere I found ;
My future looked so hopeful, sooth to say,

It seemed the dawning of a cloudless day ;
And if the Lord could e'er such lot design
For man on earth, I might have thought it mine.
But He, supreme in wisdom as in love,
Foresees the perils which His saints must prove,
If tribulation from His sovereign hand,
In mercy and unerring judgment planned,
Were not appointed, safely to control,
By patient suffering, every faithful soul !
Through this alone, the grace to pray is given,
"Thy will be done on earth, as 't is in Heaven."
Through this alone, conviction must descend,
That we for all things on His power depend.
Through this we learn to know our Father's rod,
And bow submissive to the hand of God ;
Assured that sins and woes at last shall cease,
In His bright world of purity and peace.

And here I pause ; although perhaps I may
Resume my labor at some future day.
The years of my Episcopate have been
Full thirty-three, in which the Church has seen
A fair increase, though much of my own life
Has passed in toil, not always free from strife.
My work of authorship, which soon began,
Through many books of controversy ran.
Domestic joys and sorrows had their part,
At times to cheer, at times depress my heart.

And yet I knew on whom to cast my care ;
In each event the Saviour's hand was there !
I would not choose, in all the varied range,
Had I the right, my personal lot to change ;
For though mysterious oft, the whole design,
I humbly trust, was marked by love divine.

And now, the grateful subject of His power,
So blessed in this, my GOLDEN WEDDING hour,
What other supplication can arise
To Him, the Ruler of the earth and skies,
Than this : that He, whose gracious hand has
        shed
Such favors on my own unworthy head,
May guide the little period that remains,
To the last end of mortal cares and pains ;
Write in His Book of Life each precious name
Which in my heart's affections holds its claim ;
Teach every humble soul in faith to prove
The wondrous treasure of the Saviour's love ;
And bring them all, by grace in mercy given,
With glorious triumph to His home in Heaven !

www.ingramcontent.com/pod-product-compliance
Lightning Source LLC
Chambersburg PA
CBHW032016010726
47493CB00007B/2425